I0584196

MANUEL MAGALLANES MOURE

What is Love

translated and with an afterword by
Jessica Sequeira

THIS IS A SNUGGLY BOOK

Translation and Afterword
Copyright © 2022 by Jessica Sequeira.
All rights reserved.

ISBN: 978-1-64525-109-5

What is Love

MANUEL MAGALLANES MOURE was born on November 8, 1878 in La Serena, Chile. He studied at the Escuela de Bellas Artes to become a painter, and wrote journalism for *El Mercurio* and *Las Últimas Noticias*, among other publications. He was best known to his contemporaries, however, as a poet. Along with Pedro Prado, Baldomero Lillo, Augusto D'Halmar and others, he formed part of Los Diez, one of the most famous Chilean cultural groups of the 20th century. He was a judge for the Juegos Florales literary prize awarded to Gabriela Mistral in 1914, and the two began a correspondence and complicated friendship that endured for several decades. That same year, he published the stories of *Qué es amor* (What is Love). For many years he lived in San Bernardo, where he also served as mayor, and he died there on January 19, 1924.

JESSICA SEQUEIRA was born in San Jose, California in 1989, and currently lives in Santiago de Chile. Her works include the novel *A Furious Oyster* (Dostoyevsky Wannabe), and the collection of essays *Other Paradises: Poetic Approaches to Thinking in a Technological Age* (Zero). Her translations include Adolfo Couve's *When I Think of My Missing Head* (Snuggly) and Liliana Colanzi's *Our Dead World* (Dalkey Archive).

Contents

What is Love

I'd like to write your name as the dedication to this sentimental little book. But how can I do so if I don't know your name, friend of mine . . . ?

M. MAGALLANES MOURE

The many waters could not quench love,
nor could the rivers drown it.

SOLOMON
Song of Songs
Chapter 8 verse 7

Do not say: from this water I shall not drink.

POPULAR PROVERB

What is Love?

I

"Anthony and Pachomius saw apparitions, which it isn't necessary to understand as temptations . . . The daughter of Satan didn't manifest herself to them incarnate, but only in the form of a ghost. On this point the texts are clear."

As she read in a drawling voice without inflections, the words flowed from her lips like a continuous trickle of water.

"She isn't a real being, as in the stories of Ephrem, Polycarp, Serapion or the countless other solitary figures who witnessed the approach of the temptress."

Leaning over the table crammed with papers, he followed the lines with his pen, noting letters and words, making signs and references, delaying at times to insert a complete phrase the typesetter had overlooked. Then the trickle of speech cut off abruptly and the machines' inner noise clattered into the silence of the little room. Until the reading started again, and once more the pen began to move over the printed lines.

Antonio hadn't been working for very long with the manager's daughter on the correction of proofs. Previously he'd had a young boy as assistant who was shy and docile, so much so he never reacted badly to Antonio's observations or the dressings down of the manager, a man who feigned a sickening sweetness before customers, but was full of cutting remarks and demands in his relations with employees. Antonio had been content with the boy; unfortunately, a bout of pneumonia did away with him in under a week. That's when Don Enrique decided his daughter Paulina would help Antonio with the monotonous work.

At the start, the change of colleague produced a deep unease in the mood of the corrector of proofs. He felt annoyed and self-conscious in the presence of those calm eyes, those thick lips at times finely pursed and at times smooth, soft, moist. He was made uncomfortable by the sight of that lush black hair, those plump hands, that tight-fitting bodice without any decoration, and those long oppressive skirts, too long for Paulina's age but not enough to conceal her little high-heeled boots, worn-out at the heels. The presence of all this annoyed him, not because it was unpleasant to look at, but because such details were a frightening combination for his timid spirit: because all of this constituted a woman.

To have a woman before him, to see her day after day, to work with her in that enclosed space, to talk with her, to listen to her at every moment, seemed to him an unbearable torture. He knew all too well that Paulina, in her appearance and manners, was more like a boy than a girl. Even so, to spend the hours in the company of a woman dampened his spirits, as if he were expecting some unhappiness.

The new job had no effect whatsoever on Paulina. From a young age she'd been used to contact with press employees. The men treated her like a colleague and she fraternized with them all, taking great efforts with her work. Her soul had been molded in this environment, and her figure was the image of her soul. She lived as if ignorant of her sex, indifferent to those capricious pruderies of girls that so often are no more than calls to malice, hidden signals to attract the attentions of men. She was a woman because she'd been born a woman; but her intentions weren't feminine, she didn't know how to be a woman.

II

The Catholic Press went through a period of great activity. Since the printing of religious works—and that was the house specialty—didn't result in many assignments, faced with the shortage of orders, Don Enrique had filled out applications to edit a work for the Ministry of Finance, an extremely long report about saltpeter, highly embellished with appendices, notes and extra documents. He won approval for the proposal and set his sights toward quickly finishing up the large print run.

The extra business was appreciated, but great effort was needed to get the edition out on time. The job had to be delivered before October was over—and the first two weeks had already passed.

So Don Enrique worked feverishly. Since his usual employees weren't able to handle the job on their own, he found it necessary to hire others. From the first hours of morning until nightfall, the presses clattered away without a break. Neither machines nor men enjoyed any rest. A loud droning noise constantly filled the press, a buzzing to which at times Don Enrique added his voice, shouting orders or issuing reprimands. Inside, all was movement. The pulleys rushed in search of axles, the toothed wheels rotated and slotted their gears together; the steel arms rose and fell in rhythm; the paper moved forward until the shapes pressed against it; and the printed folds, damp and smelling of oil, fell smoothly, one over the other, forming mountains that speedily piled up.

Yet the unusual activity didn't reach the isolated little room where the correction of proofs took place. Among the just hired employees were two copyeditors in charge of overseeing the extraordinary labor required to print the ministerial report.

Antonio and Paulina were able to keep relatively calm in the midst of such frenzied work.

The unpleasant impression the girl's presence made on Antonio at first had begun to disappear little by little. He grew used to Paulina's company and even dared to furtively glance at her. He looked at her briefly, and then, a little more confident, he rested his gaze for longer moments on that face that wasn't beautiful, but was full of gentleness. Once, while raising his gaze from the printed paper, his eyes met hers and her eyes also looked into his. Then Antonio experienced a shiver, a sensation that made his soul fold back toward its depths, just as the antenna of a snail draws back at the slightest contact.

And now, amongst the eternal religious pages—Catholic publications, lives of saints, mystic pamphlets, books of prayers—something new livened up the heap of monotonous and serious productions. It was the proofs of a literary magazine, that although edited by conservative youths from San Ignacio Academy, often slipped some words into its columns with a view toward the exterior life, some naïvely amorous verses, some story with a scent of humanity.

Paulina's pale voice took on color at times, acquired inflections, emphasized certain phrases; she interpreted different passages from the reading with modulations she hadn't possessed before. Antonio, for his part, almost paid no attention to the printed page as he listened to what was said by those thick lips, which she constantly moistened, as if to savor the words.

III

The period for the delivery of the official edition was reaching its end. The activity of the press took on greater intensity. The workers, sweating, did their jobs in silence, as the machines stepped up their pace, and in the workshops the air overheated from such prolonged labor, as spring sent its first waves of heat through the city, was intense, enervating.

Ever since the correction of the magazine's proofs had been entrusted to them, Antonio and Paulina had made efforts to get through the other, more religious pages as quickly as possible, with the incessant repetitions of the more pious and plaintive articles turning into an annoyance.

"Twenty pages of the *Straight Path to Reach Heaven*. Should we look at that first?"

Antonio asked:

"And what else is there?"

"A page of the magazine."

"Let's finish off the *Straight Path*," said Antonio, with the voice of a sacristan, "then we'll see to the magazine."

Paulina read hastily, without waiting for Antonio to catch up with his scrawls.

They polished off twenty pages of the mystical book in a moment.

"Now the magazine."

They settled into their seats, as if preparing to better receive and enjoy its pleasure.

Face to face, they were separated by the narrow table.

Paulina took the originals of the magazine and placed them before her, and Antonio did the same with the printed sheet. Then the reading began.

It was a somewhat vapid article about morality in the theater, something the author demanded of playwrights as an indispensable condition for the creation of a lasting work.

The voice of Paulina, slow and warm at the beginning, grew rapid once more. This didn't live up to her expectations.

Afterward came a story translated from French, then some verses from Italian.

"What is Love?"

That was the title of the composition.

Paulina's voice trembled a little as she spoke the words. Antonio leaned over the table.

The verses that followed were musical and deep:

Virginal faces:
What is love,
how to earn its laurels you ask,
dedicated and serious . . .
Ah! the tyrannous lord of souls
is mystery, mystery,
mystery

Paulina went quiet, as Antonio jotted a correction in the margin. It was necessary to read the verses again. Paulina started to read, but this time, all at once, her voice broke off. Her foot, anxious, restless, had just bumped into Antonio's, a soft and gentle graze that made something inside her give way.

They looked at one another. The eyes of the young woman rested on those of the young man, which were calm, with an increasing gleam within their depths. He lowered his head, disturbed. His beard shook slightly.

Paulina went on:

Like lightning
that descends swift
upon the raised imploring chest,
a disturbance;
or a careful thief who penetrates
so quietly, quietly,
quietly

Her voice went mute again. Now she read to herself, barely moving her lips. Antonio waited with pen on paper, not daring to raise his eyes. In his temples, two little veins had begun to pulse. At last, when he resolved to look up, he found Paulina's eyes fixed upon him.

Although he didn't make the slightest movement, he had the sensation he was leaning back to avoid falling into an abyss. The girl smiled. It was a forced smile, nearly a gesture of pain. Her plump hand advanced, dragging itself over the paper, and clasped Antonio's.

Still looking into each other's eyes, she smiling with pain, he with a hypnotized expression, they stretched their necks forward to join their mouths in a languid kiss, a long kiss that clouded their eyes and gave infinite pleasure to their whole being.

When the vertigo passed, Don Enrique's voice, over the complicated racket of machines, was shouting furiously.

New Year

I

As he left La Moneda[1], after making quick work of his few tasks that day, the last of the year, Daniel Prado glanced at the clock on the Ministry of War building.

Three forty-five.

He had the entire afternoon free.

What to do? Where to go?

Before reaching the corner he made his decision: he'd take a tram and go see Marta. Ah, what a delightful prospect! He'd arrive at the hour for tea, and stay with her until evening. Then he'd go home, eat with his wife and little ones, and remain there in expectation of the midnight cannon shot that announced the new year.

---

1 La Moneda Palace is where the President of Chile has his office; many government workers are also based there.

He passed a gondola carriage, happily waving its little canvas curtains in the wind, and without taking the precaution of signaling to the conductor to slow down, he made an agile leap to board the tram. The sun bathed the street from wall to wall, and gave a shine to the paving stones polished by traffic. An enormous bunch of white flowers swooned at the feet of a well-known image of the Conception, raising her eyes to the sky behind a grille a short distance from the ground, at the entrance to a certain pious house. Along the length of the sun-warmed walls, one window followed another, all closed, all opposing their white shutters to the invasion of that too vivid, too ardent light.

The windows of Marta's house were closed too, so that when Daniel entered the little sitting room where he was used to being received, his eyes, still dazzled by the outside brightness, were overwhelmed by the semi-darkness. But he was well acquainted with the arrangement of furniture in that pleasant room, and without great effort, he immediately found the wide armchair in his favorite corner.

Soon, in the glints of a thin ray of light that stretched out the length of the hallway, he began to distinguish some objects familiar to him: the little central table in a Louis XV style, with the metal tray to receive cards and the pot of artificial flowers; the varnished sideboard of bibelots; the photographs in gold frames whose glass copied and deformed them; the black and red geometric patterns of the sun-covered floor tiles.

Then he heard those idling steps without haste, whose slow shuffle put happiness into his soul, and shortly afterward, there was the tall shadow of Marta in the doorway, blocking the ray of sun.

Even when she realized that Daniel was there, she remained for a moment without moving, without entering, hesitating at the edge of the dark room. Then he went toward her and grabbed her hand which fell beside her skirt, a soft, gentle hand that let itself be held with no resistance.

Both smiled with languor.

"Are you alone?"

He felt a twinge of irritation when he learned that Doña Cristina was home.

"She's here," insisted Marta, "and it won't be long before she comes to greet you."

It was a warning to remain prudent. He contented himself with squeezing the docile hand again and going to his corner, while she opened the window of the patio a crack so that more light could enter. How interested they were in keeping up appearances! As if their expectations of happiness rested on such hypocrisy. They knew well that Doña Cristina suspected something, that she spied on them with the aim of confirming her suspicions, and that for this reason it was necessary for them to be constantly alert, not growing careless for even a moment.

Marta had said so to Daniel many times, in the delightful intimacy of their asides:

"Do you think I'm frightened by the idea of Juan de Dios realizing? No! What scares me is that my Mama will find out . . . You don't know what she's like."

And he'd concluded by thinking like Marta, to the extreme that it didn't matter to him overly much to commit a few imprudent acts in front of her husband.

Now, after learning that Doña Cristina was home and that she wouldn't take long to show up, Daniel stayed mute, his eyes fixed on the wall before him. Marta, for her part, spoke with deliberate seriousness of things without interest.

Light footsteps were heard running through the hallway, and shortly afterward a small child erupted into the sitting room. Crossing the threshold, she tripped and fell flat on her face in the room.

"For heaven's sake, my girl!"

Throwing out her arms, Marta ran to go pick up the girl, who whimpered as she tried to hold back her tears, although she hadn't hurt herself. As Daniel moved forward, so did Marta, and their hands met, and their heads were together, and their eyes and their lips were close, very close: but even though they looked at each other with love, they lacked the resolution to join their lips in the kiss they'd both desired for a long time. The fear that Doña Cristina would suddenly appear held them back.

Daniel went back to his corner. Marta, in the meantime, remained squatting, thighs clinging to the tautness of her skirt. Facing her, the little one pursed her thick lips, hands clasped behind her and starched smock flipped upward like a bell that doesn't change position even when turned over.

"Poor thing, my baby girl, what a silly fall."

And Marta started to kiss her, to crush her in a fierce hug.

Daniel contemplated mother and daughter, and curiously enough, it didn't even occur to him to think this small creature with blonde locks and dark eyes was the living testimony that Marta belonged to another man. The tenderness of the young mother won him over, and he too caressed the little one with sympathy, as if she were his own.

At that moment Doña Cristina entered, peering through the lenses of the glasses perched on her nose.

"What is it? Did something happen to the girl?"

Daniel came forward to greet her.

"Ah, how are you, Prado? I didn't know you were here."

She left her tiny work basket on the table and went up to Marta, who'd pulled the girl toward the sofa to better sit her on her skirt and cover her with caresses. The little one remained sad, as if trying to prolong such an advantageous situation with her mother, her grandmother and even Daniel himself, who in part from his own inclinations, in part to please Marta, directed affectionate words from the corner to his young friend.

Doña Cristina, leaning over her granddaughter, planted a loud kiss on her cheek, then gave a deep sniff that made her glasses-pinched nose give a whistle.

"Naughty rascal!"

She picked up her basket again and went to sit in the light, starting a conversation with Daniel which Marta soon joined.

The questions and answers were always the same:

"Your wife . . . is she well? Your girls . . . I'm so sick . . . The heart, you know, I've inherited fainting fits. And my father died from an angina. But these young ones don't believe me, they say it's just nerves . . ."

She spoke while rhythmically moving her crochet needles, stopping now and then to examine the weave and count the stitches.

"They don't believe me, Prado . . ."

"But Mama," replied Marta smiling, "how can we believe you if the doctors say you've got nothing in your heart."

Then the señora lowered her hands, and looking at Daniel over her glasses, said:

"If I didn't know her, I'd think that she wished I were dead. Her indifference is so great . . ."

"Mama, my God, don't say that."

These dialogues between mother and daughter, which arose so often, put Daniel into a difficult position, since he couldn't decide which side to take. To agree with one was to provoke the other's displeasure, and that, as he well understood, was not convenient. And so he brought all his diplomacy into play to avoid venturing a serious opinion, and as a last resort, when the discussion grew heated, he chose to smile and stay quiet.

"Ah, the two of you don't know how important a mother is . . ." he joked.

Señora Cristina spoke of her ailments, a topic that easily moved her, to the point her restless eyes blinked and grew watery.

Marta, now free of the little one, winked at Daniel.

"She's so ill, yet she doesn't take the medicines the doctor prescribes to her . . ."

One morning, when Doña Cristina had complained about her poor state of health, Daniel had asked if she'd taken the ferric sesquibromide pills prescribed by the doctor.

"Every day, Prado, every day . . . And I'm going to take them now, before I forget."

They were in the sewing room, next to the señora's bedroom. Daniel resolved to confirm a suspicion that had nagged at him for some time now . . . From his concealed position, he observed all of Doña Cristina's movements. The wily señora pulled out a jangling bunch of keys from her pocket, loudly opened her upper dresser drawer, sank her hand inside it as if looking for something, closed it again and headed for her nightstand. She grabbed the bottle of water, poured out half a glass and drank it down. Afterward she put the glass up-side-down over the bottle. Daniel smiled from his observation point: it was as he'd suspected. Doña Cristina had perfectly simulated the act of taking the pills, only she'd forgotten the movement of bringing them to her mouth. The next day, in a moment when he found himself alone with Marta, Daniel told her what he'd seen. The beautiful woman laughed with him, saying:

"You don't have to tell me . . . She's always been like this, my mother. Don't you see she plays sick just so we'll pamper her? The funniest thing is Juan de Dios believes her . . . Poor Juan de Dios!"

Ever since then, Marta had made allusions to Daniel's discovery in her dialogues with Doña Cristina, with the gleeful aim of making her friend feel uncomfortable. The señora, without imagining she'd been found out, protested with exaggeration:

"What do you know, silly girl! I wish I had all the money back that doctors have made me spend on medicines . . . I'd have enough to buy a three-story palace."

II

When they finished taking tea, Marta proposed moving to the living room. The sun was already setting, and by opening up the balcony, they could breathe some fresh air.

"Mama, the heat isn't good for you. And we can watch the people in the street. Let's go?"

Without waiting for Doña Cristina's reply, Marta made her way to the dining room, feigning the most indifferent expression in the world. Her tall body advanced with languid movements. For a moment she stopped in the hallway before the door, hands clasped behind her, tight provocative bust pushed out, little head raised, dark green eyes turned upward, and red mouth twisting continuously into new shapes, in a delectable game.

In passing, she'd plucked up a sugar lump and was now entertaining herself giving it turns as she sucked it, letting a corner of the white sweet be glimpsed on occasion between the crimson of her full shiny lips.

Then, as Doña Cristina made no gesture to get up, she cried out, while still looking at the sky:

"I'd say it's an airplane . . ."

The simple phrase had an excellent effect. The good señora stood up in haste and went to look. Daniel followed behind her. But at that moment, Marta, feigning distress, said:

"Oh, how silly I am! It's only a bird!"

And she walked on through to the living room.

By the time Daniel and Doña Cristina reached the vast room, Marta had already opened the balcony doors. The upper parts of the facing buildings were soaked in orange light, harmonizing with the blue shadow cut into architectural shapes that served as their limit. The living room was inundated by shimmering flecks of gold.

Doña Cristina carried an easy chair out to the balcony and settled in to one side, so that she could observe without being seen from below. Daniel, against his wishes, sank into the sofa inside; but perhaps Marta considered this to be an excess of prudence, for she didn't take long to call out:

"Come to the balcony . . . You can breathe better here."

Doña Cristina had picked up her crochet, and was toiling away once again at the work.

Daniel got up at the very moment that a hoarse whirring approached, over which there soared the muffled clanging of a bell. Cutting through the varied buzzing of the street and the slight trembling of glass, the big blue elongated shadow of an electric tram went by, crammed with passengers whose silhouettes, in the swiftness of their motion, also elongated into horizontal bands.

Marta glanced at Doña Cristina and quickly said to Daniel:

"Let's take advantage of the noise."

And fixing her caressing eyes on him:

"Will you always want to believe in it?"

"Forever, Marta. You have no reason to doubt."

They changed the conversation because just then, the tram stopped at the nearby corner and Doña Cristina could hear them.

"What a world of people!"

"As if everyone wanted to end the year by going out . . ."

A silence, then:

"What do you prefer, Prado: Christmas or New Year?"

"New Year, Señora."

"Why? Christmas is so wonderful!"

"But Christmas doesn't bring me bonuses, while New Year . . ."

"Brings them?"

"Brings hope, at least."

"But . . . what could you hope for that you don't already have?"

"Ah! So many things . . ."

Doña Cristina interrupted, without raising her eyes from her work:

"Men are never satisfied."

"But Señora, who doesn't hope for something more than what he's already got?"

"I, Prado, no longer hope for anything, not even health."

Marta smiled at Daniel, making a spiteful gesture.

"How do you know, mother, that next year . . ."

"They won't bury me, is that it?"

"Oh! It's impossible to talk with you."

Another tram approached, and as the señora grumbled from her easy chair, they resumed their intimate dialogue, in which if words said much, gazes and smiles said even more.

"Do you believe me? Tell me you believe me!"

"You're just as bad as she is . . ."

"Ask me for proof."

"Proof?" Her gaze was vague, as if in a dream. "No, Daniel. We're being crazy."

"And are we to blame for that?"

While her eyes moved quickly, following each window of the tram, she said with
seriousness:

"If you were single at least . . . maybe it
wouldn't be so mad. But like this, married,
with children . . ."

It was an objection that unsettled Daniel
and made him fall silent, a circumstance she
took advantage of to insist again, as if hoping
he'd find an argument that cut the ground from
beneath her scruples.

"Don't you think I'm right?"

Yes, he thought, she was right, but only
to a point. If he were a rogue, a scoundrel,
one of those husbands who look for another
woman's love because they've never felt affection for their own, then Marta's observation
would be justified. But he wasn't like that, nor
was the love he felt for her a consequence of
any lack of affection for his wife. No; in the
noble ingenuousness of his soul, Daniel swore
to himself that his passion for Marta, formed
through many months of respectful friendship,
would not have to reduce in the slightest the
tender esteem, the calm affection inspired in
him by his Adela. He felt capable of loving
the one without ceasing to care for the other;
he considered the affections to be two streams

that ran in parallel without ever mixing their waters, without ever moving away from one another too much, and which went to empty themselves in the same blue lake, without making a noise, without raising scandal, with barely the laughing murmur that a current produces in the stillness of quiet water. That blue lake was happiness, the gentle happiness of loving calmly, and without limitation, these two women whom he, considering them separately, compared to the two parts into which a sculptor friend of his divided the mold of a figure in the process of casting; two parts that when joined gave shape to a single and very beautiful sculpture. Like that sculptor, Daniel united the two women in his imagination, and from their union, perfect and sublime, the incarnation of his ideal emerged.

It began to grow dark. The electric lights along the street, hanging in a swaying rosary, blinked; inside the white glass globes were flutterings of violet light, then all at once, like a suddenly focused gaze, a steady brightness fell onto the blue shadow below.

The trams also lit their golden lamps, and as they went by the intertwined shadows of Daniel and Marta started to move over the wall, dropped onto the living room's red rug, passed impudently over Doña Cristina—who settled in her easy chair, now dedicated herself to silent contemplation of the traffic—then crushed themselves once more against another wall, broke on the architectural projections, ran off in fantastic flight and dissolved at last in white light, half a block away.

Leaning on the balcony as they spoke in secret, Daniel had little by little moved his foot forward until it touched Marta's, which didn't move away. The shadow on the ground was in their favor. They pretended to look with great interest to one side, as if something extraordinary were coming from that way, then one of them turned abruptly in the opposite direction: their gazes met, and they remained looking at one another for a brief moment, penetrating each other to the depths, at the same time as their feet pressed against each other's with greater force.

"Ask me for proof if you doubt . . ."

"So it'll be like Christmas, when you didn't do what I asked of you."

"No Marta, not now. Whatever you ask of me, I'll do."

She gave a faint smile.

"Are you sure . . . Whatever I ask . . . ?"

He answered gravely.

"Whatever you ask of me."

"Alright. Tonight at twelve you'll go to the Plaza de las Armas and look for me, to give me a New Year's embrace."

"And what if I don't find you in the chaos?"

"You'll find me, or rather, I'll find you."

"How?"

"It's simple. Wait for me ten minutes before twelve in the part of the plaza facing the post office. I'll go by with Juan de Dios, and you'll follow behind, pretending you haven't seen me. When the cannon goes off . . ."

"I'll catch up to you?"

"No, I'll turn around and then we'll meet each other . . . face to face."

III

The dinner was joyful yet calm, as occurs when people don't need to hide their unhappy spirits with loud noise.

All the food was served quickly. Adela had given the staff permission to visit the movie theater, and since the film started at nine, they had to be free soon.

"And what about us, Mommy . . . when are we going to the 'mothiveter'?" innocently asked one of the little ones, the dark one who looked like her mother, opening her big eyes.

"When, mommy?" the blonde asked in turn, fixing an eloquent gaze on Daniel.

"Tomorrow a gentleman will take you to the *matinée*."

"What gentleman, Mama?"

"One who's good to you when you behave yourselves."

And the girl with blue eyes asked:

"Grandma's gentleman, Mommy?"

Grandma's gentleman was a character invented by Adela's kindhearted mother to help educate the little ones. How could Adela reprimand them for such a question? It was true that their dear grandmother, with an expression of mystery and in a restrained voice, had told them that very early one morning in the street, while leaving the church, she'd met a gentleman who'd told her more or less: "Señora, I've seen your grandchildren playing in the sun without their hats. That's not good, for they'll get sick and you'll have to give them some very nasty medicines." Other times, the neatly dressed elderly lady arrived with a package, and after questioning the girls for a long time, who answered as if in a dream without taking their eyes off of it, she handed it over to the older one, the angelic blonde. When the package was opened in feverish haste, two pink celluloid dolls appeared with their corresponding factory brands stamped on the buttock. It was a gift sent to them by the gentleman, as a reward for good behavior. The good gentleman! How respectable everything he said was, and what an effort he made to please little girls who behaved themselves!

"Grandma's gentleman, Mommy?"

Adela smiled and turned her big dark eyes toward Daniel.

"Ah! Papa!" said the dark little one, with eyes lit up.

"Yes, Papa!" repeated the blonde, jumping with happiness.

"Yes, me!" announced Daniel, contemplating them with affection. "And now off to bed, so tomorrow you can wake up early."

"Will you give us a kiss tonight when the cannon goes off? Mama said you would . . ."

Daniel had to disguise the unease this comment by the little ones gave him.

"Yes, yes."

And he said no more.

Adela went out with the little girls and he stayed there reading the afternoon newspaper, trying to take an interest in the political news and cables from abroad, without managing to keep his mind away from the somewhat confused idea of what he was going to do later on.

For a moment his imagination let itself be captured by the new account given by an English correspondent of an episode from the Balkan Wars. But when he'd concluded the paragraph, the vague unease of a short time before weighed down his soul again. He stood and went to the bedroom.

Adela had already put the little ones to bed, and now she lit the lamp on the marble dressing table, behind a pitcher of water that served as its shade.

She spoke in a low voice.

"Will you stay here for a bit while I go settle with the servants?"

He nodded yes, and Adela tiptoed out.

Daniel approached the little ones' beds, listened to the gentle and regular sound of their breathing, then stretched out on the wide matrimonial bed between the sleeping creatures. He stared at the ceiling gently illuminated by the lamp's trembling light. Point by point, he began to remember his afternoon visit to Marta. He felt a disturbing pleasure as he reproduced in his imagination the delicious impression it had given to him to squeeze, in his feverish hand, the cool and soft one of his friend. With the vividness of reality, he once again experienced the sensation he'd felt as his foot vigorously brushed against her delicate one, as in an act of possession. Again there passed before his eyes, moving something in his soul, those slow gazes of her green eyes and those caressing smiles of her full puckered lips, which seemed to ask him for a sweet and endless kiss. Once again he saw the tall lazy woman with hands clasped behind her, provocative bust thrust forward, little head raised . . . And the indefinable unease that had weighed on him a short time before started to clear, like a mist dissipated by wind. He'd decided now: he'd go where Marta had told him she'd be waiting; he'd leave his wife and his little girls for a moment. "After all," he thought, "it isn't about abandoning Adela, or taking away from her a scrap of the affection I've given her. It's good to shake up the prejudices a little, to release oneself from tyranny, to break a few rings of the chain the masses insist on fastening to themselves." The entire conflict was over in just a few minutes. Would he love his wife any less because instead of giving her a kiss at twelve, he gave it to her at eleven thirty or twelve fifteen? He smiled with a scornful gesture, satisfied by his reasoning. "How foolish most people are, my God! Anyway, does the year really end when the song of the last chime dies out at twelve? What about the clocks in Europe? Fiddlesticks!"

He sat up when he felt Adela come in, circled his arm around her waist and kissed her mouth.

"Are you free at last?"

And she, breathing out:

"At last . . ."

"Then let's go to the living room. I want to hear you play something. The 'Vals d'Amour' by Moszkowsky, how about it?"

He felt light, content. A little more and he'd have kicked his heels together in a happy caper.

He sat next to the piano and opened his soul to the warm music of the Russian composer[1], which Adela interpreted in a passionate style.

By a phenomenon of musical evocation quite frequent in him, that waltz always brought before his eyes the vision of Emma

---

1 Moritz Moszkowski (1854-1925) was a German composer of Polish-Jewish descent, so this is a possible error by Magallanes Moure. It is true that Russia was much romanticized by the writer and his artistic colleagues—as in their attempt to found a Tolstoyan colony, for instance—and thus to name a Russian composer was profoundly evocative. On the other hand, Magallanes Moure may have been attempting to express the superficial artistic knowledge of his protagonist.

Bovary, swept along by her companion into a vertigo of speed and sensuality. He remembered the admirable phrases of Flaubert: "*Ils commencèrent lentement, puis allèrent plus vite.*" And then: "*En passant auprès des portes, la robe d'Emma, par le bas, sériflait au pantalon; leurs jambes entraint l'une dans l'autre; il baissait ses regards vers elle, elle levait les siens vers lui . . .*" He knew the living fragment by heart.

"How about you play something by Grieg now?"

She chose "Jour de Noces"[1], the joyful springtime composition by the pale old Norwegian. He saw how the wedding procession was ushered into being, advancing along a path skirted by trees dressed in new leaves, headed by enthusiastic violins. Ah, the simple happiness of villagers in love!

Adela's face radiated the freshness given to her spirit by the wholesome music. Her dark eyes were illuminated, and a swift and graceful smile appeared on her slightly open mouth. The movements of her flexible bust moved in rhythm with her toccata's dancing beat: her expressive hands were sometimes nervously energetic, other times tenderly languid; her tight-fitting skirt formed a mold of her legs and

---

1 Also known as "Wedding Day at Troldhaugen".

betrayed with slender folds the poignant hollow of her lap. Every now and then, when the performance allowed it, one of her hands left the keyboard and with a rapid gesture pushed back a curl of brown hair that had stubbornly fallen over her face.

The night passed imperceptibly for both of them: Adela, devoted to the growing pleasure of translating into piano the tenderness in her soul of a wife in love; Daniel, happy in the contemplation of this woman who was his, as well as in his imagination of the other . . . the beautiful friend who, taking advantage of tradition, had promised him an embrace in the face of her husband and the entire town.

There was a moment when Adela, after concluding the interpretation of a passage by Schumann, stopped to flip through the album in search of another composition.

Since Daniel remained absorbed in his thoughts, she questioned him:

"Hello! Are you sleepy?"

He smiled blissfully:

"Sleepy? Why would you think that!"

At that moment, the clock in the dining room struck up the simple melody of its strokes, and from that harmonious prelude there came away, slow and light, like drops of light in shadow, eleven chimes.

"Do you hear that?" she exclaimed.

"Yes, it's eleven."

"And I still haven't heated the water! What time will the tea be ready now?"

She took down the sheets of music, closed the piano lid, offered Daniel her lips as she passed, and went out saying:

"I'll be right back . . ."

For a moment he heard her light steps on the parquet of the hallway, then all was silent . . .

Leaning back in his chair with arms crossed, one leg resting on the other and gently balancing his foot, Daniel looked for a way to go out without awakening suspicion in his wife. Now that he was close to the action, the vague unease he'd experienced moments before came back to weigh on him. For a brief moment, he gave up the idea of leaving Adela alone in those last moments of the year, which had always found them together. His spirits shrank from the thought that for the first time, he was going to break the old and beautiful custom. Then he thought of leaving the agreeable stillness, where he was, to fling himself into the street and across the city . . .

Some people passed in a hurry, and amongst the murmur of voices that went with them, Daniel heard the tones of a feminine voice rise up:

"Not to the Plaza for anything, I don't want everyone to hug me . . ."

Daniel couldn't make out any other words, but by the tones of the men who were moving away, he understood they were trying to convince the lady to accompany them.

He stayed there looking at the closed shutters, and again there appeared in his mind the image of Marta, fixing her green eyes on him, smiling at him with her full shining lips, asking in an affectionate voice:

"Will you always want to believe in it?"

He took off his watch and contemplated its white face where a tiny bit of metal rotated, set in red enamel with little characters that said: "*Toujours*", a gift Marta had presented to him one afternoon they were alone in the living room, until the lamps turned on.

After this he stood up, resolute.

He found Adela in the dining room, preparing the table for midnight tea.

As soon as she saw him come in, she said in a joking tone:

"Have you come to hurry me along?"

Daniel gave her an effortless smile.

"No, just the opposite. I've come to tell you not to serve it yet, since I'm going to buy sweets . . ."

"I forgot them, you're right. But at this time . . . It's just twenty-five minutes to twelve."

She spoke these last words with a pleading expression, an obsequious gesture.

Then he approached her, still smiling, and taking hold of her head with both his hands, he pressed his mouth against hers in a long, firm kiss full of promises.

"I'll be to the Alameda and back before you know it."

Adela managed to become serious.

"If you're not back before twelve . . ."

And she stayed there with hands fallen, looking at the door through which he'd gone out.

For a brief moment, Daniel hesitated between leaving and coming in again. The night was calm, the sky strewn with trembling stars. He observed the silent street. In the distance the red lights of a carriage danced, jolted in its passage by the bumps of the pavement. Under the streetlight in that half block, a few pale dresses were briefly illuminated, disappearing once again into shadow. Then a murmur of far-away voices came to him, the drawn-out song of a vendor.

He shut the door with care, and began to walk.

There was enough time to reach the Plaza at the hour Marta had indicated. But unconsciously he hastened his step, taking pleasure in the fresh breeze descending in gentle waves from the cordillera to the city.

On his way he passed many households that were still awake in anticipation of the New Year. There were half-open doors with talkative neighbors seated on the doorstep and the round light of a Chinese lantern in the distance behind them; passages lit by a thick strip of brilliance from some side door; luminous windows and hallways and echoes of delighted voices that gave life to everything, snatches of laughter, quick feminine shouts.

The joy of these lively houses made his own rise up in his mind, closed, dark and silent just as he'd seen it before he walked away, and the evocation brought a mist of melancholy to his spirit. He thought of Adela . . . He tried to remember how the two of them had spent the final night of the previous year, and walking, always walking, he reconstructed with fragmentary images the placid vision of that intimate evening so similar to the one he'd just interrupted with his abrupt departure. What serene joy he'd felt in that happy time, at once so near and so distant, when his soul still hadn't known the conflict of opposing sentiments, and the longings of his heart were in complete agreement, like waters in a tranquil current!

At the corner of the Alameda he had to stop because the traffic of vehicles made crossing difficult. He looked to one side, then the other, dazzled by the blinding flash of an automobile's headlights as it sprinted toward Central Station, skimming the ground like a big cockroach with shining eyes.

Daniel crossed the road and continued down the middle of the avenue toward Ahumada Street. Distractedly he ran his eyes over the jumbled groups of grotesque drunks, indigenous women adorned with flowers, spruced-up provincials, insignificant townspeople with loud comments about the fireworks or how they were going to wait at the foot of Santa Lucía hill[1] for the twelve o'clock cannon shot. The comings and goings of the crowd had spread over the promenade a floating cloud of dust, which took on iridescent glints as it absorbed the greenish light of gas burners, the bluish brightness of electric lamps, or the golden glow of shop lanterns.

Ahumada Street looked more narrow than usual with the flood of passersby. From the

1 The cerro Santa Lucía is located at the center of Santiago, overlooking the city's major avenue.

wide door of the movie theater hall, illuminated *a giorno*, a human torrent overflowed into the street, through which Daniel, with sidesteps and squeezes, was able to open a path. As he passed he heard the shout: "Bye, Prado!" repeated several times. It was a group of friends, and so as not to find himself obliged to continue on with them, he quickened his step.

Shining victoria carriages rolled along, led by the long strides of gleaming horses, and the feathers of the elegant ones traveling inside them, flamboyant ladies wrapped in filmy pale dresses who looked like big flowers, swayed in the wind. The automobiles sped away, and as they glided some let out strangled chokes like the hoarse cries of roosters that one grabs by the neck, while others trumpeted loudly or attacked the four notes of a hunting toccata. All left behind them the ticklish fumes of gasoline.

Daniel's restless spirit felt it expanded when the Plaza de Armas came into view, full of lights and animation, a large multicolored swarm slowly circulating around a bush. As he approached, he noticed that the public had formed two concentric circles, doing turns in opposite directions like girandola fireworks. A constant murmur, similar to the buzzing of bees around flowering branches, rose from that festive crowd, and above the dizzying noise, like threads of gold in dark cloth, the scandalous motifs of a fashionable operetta stood out, played at full tilt by a teeming band of musicians.

Daniel took out his watch. Eleven forty-five. He'd made it in time.

He moved along the edge of the promenade, picking his way between the onlookers in a tight column under the trees that lined the sidewalk, afraid he'd be stopped by some overly affectionate friend and examining with vigilant eye the confusion of elegant women, in the midst of whom would be Marta, luxurious, distinguished, majestic like a queen. Between the trees, the Council clock showed its hanging disc, up high, palely illuminated like a moon made for the stage. The shadowy pointers indicated eleven forty-five. Had time stopped moving? In front of the post office he halted and positioned himself next to a tree trunk, in the darkness. His gaze turned itself to exploring, with unflagging exhaustiveness, the bustle of the crowd. Lifting his head slightly, beard raised up, he turned his eyes to the flowing of the human current. The groups of fashionably dressed women appeared as an incessant stream, the bubbling of a spring, and Daniel's gaze pinned itself to those flowery groups, moved along with them, followed them and returned when he convinced himself Marta wasn't among them, and then accompanied them for another long stretch, if he made out a feather or a chiffon headdress a little taller than the rest. That's Marta! said the shudder of emotion that took hold of his soul. But every time the lofty plume or upright chiffon approached, he sank into the realization that his eyes and soul had deceived him.

He looked at the luminous disc of the old tower. Eleven fifty-two. What a long wait!

The buzzing of the crowd increased, the voices and laughter became louder, and people seemed to parade by with greater lightness. From time to time tremulous waves came to him on which there swayed a waltz's languid rhythm, a sigh from the band of musicians.

The happy, laughing or simply captivated faces of the passersby began to produce a tickle of irritation in Daniel's mood. Those superficial girls and young men in tailored suits are laughing and laughing, he thought, because they've never known the severe joy of profound love, and have never felt true happiness, the kind given only to those who have suffered much and resembles the bloom of pain. He looked with scorn at those professionals of the flirt who made a game of what was most serious in life, and concluded by pitying them all, men and women, judging them incapable of feeling a passion so intense, so deep within the soul, as the one he felt for Marta.

Little by little he'd gone about reducing the area over which his eyes traveled, limiting it to a brief space, no more than the stretch before him. The minutes slipped by; the nervous tension of a short time before was followed now by an indefinable fatigue, bordering on resignation. Then he began to make conjectures: What could it be? Could Marta perhaps be sick? But he'd seen her looking well just a few hours before, at nightfall . . . Could Juan de Dios have refused to bring her to the Plaza? No; that wasn't believable either, given the control that the imperious will of the beautiful woman exercised over the timid and indecisive man. Could it be . . . ? He stood on his tip-toes again and looked with anxiety over the heads of the crowd, whose number swelled more and more, to the extent that circulation became nearly impossible. He looked to one side, then the other: nothing, nothing.

There were just five minutes to twelve. The music had stopped; the volume of the shouts began to decrease: the crowd seemed to gather itself as before the expectation of something very solemn.

All at once, ah, what happiness! It was her at last, his beautiful Marta, his beloved! There, amidst the movement of that group . . .

He hurled himself to one side to see better; he bounded toward her, then stopped to search for her again on tiptoe. People seemed to take pleasure in hiding the slender figure of that woman from him. He couldn't see her now, she was concealed behind that human barrier raised between himself and the fugitive vision. His eyes darted without rest, like those of a dog that's lost its owner, over all the places where the glimpsed figure might appear; but his scrutiny was in vain.

Quickly he raised his eyes to look at the clock on the tower. The pointers were about to join now, on the line for twelve. He turned to scan the place where he thought he'd sighted Marta, this time with greater hope, and without warning, while he was most absorbed in his scrutiny, the boom of the cannon shot and prolonged ooh! of the crowd oppressed his soul.

The bitterness he felt at that moment! How his sadness of abandonment contrasted with the excitement of the people congratulating each other with shouts and embracing each other, laughing in joy! and how ironically did the noisy clanging of the bells, the melodious chords of the music, the horns waggishly trumpeting from the cars sound in his ears! He'd have liked to flee from there, to start running toward his house; but something stronger than this impulse kept him rooted him to the side of the road where he found himself even as the crowd began to disperse: hope, the hope of still finding Marta, of seeing her, even if only from a distance . . .

When he decided, at last! to go, only isolated groups remained in the promenade, from which there came laughter and cries of joy.

He walked with chin up, fiercely, giving way to no one. He felt a growing irritation within him against Marta. He even came to think he hated her. The deceiver!

Amidst the procession that swirled along the sidewalk, he moved like a shipwreck survivor, who in final desperation abandons himself to the current. The inner spectacle of his soul deprived him of any interest in what was happening around or outside him. With admirable precision he saw the image of Marta fixing her tranquil and caressing gaze on him, saying:

"Will you always want to believe in it?"

And through this vision, which elevated his anger into fury, he saw through blurred eyes the movement of people, the passing of trams jammed with passengers, the flight of flower-covered carriages . . .

In the Alameda now, looking distractedly at the illuminated window of a pastry shop, he remembered all at once he'd gone out under the pretense of buying sweets. Turning on his heel, he entered and bought whatever they wanted to sell him.

When he entered the tranquility of his sleepy street, he felt the sharp irritability of his soul soften and languish, as a hand tensed by passion slackens, grows flexible and becomes elastic as it begins a caress of gratitude. He remembered Adela, and the collapse of his spirit eased into tenderness.

Some houses were still awake, which again brought him the vision of his own, closed, silent. He was tormented once again imagining his wife's sad wait, the pain she must have felt when after the prelude of the clock's strokes, the twelve chimes of midnight floated up, deep and slow. It was the first time, after eight years of love, the arrival of the new year had found them separated. And he was the guilty one . . .

He reached the door of his house. Before putting the key in the lock, he listened: not a sound inside, not the murmur of a voice. In the distance, in contrast, the muffled rolling of a carriage and swinging echo of a woman's song could be heard.

Slowly he opened the door, but despite his caution it gave a weak moan. He'd hoped to find Adela still waiting for him in the dining room, and his lips pursed when he confirmed the entire house was asleep, in darkness.

On tiptoe, he entered the bedroom. Adela had gone to bed. In the trembling gleam of the lamp he saw the dark patch of her head on a pillow. Was she really asleep? He listened more closely, and for all his efforts he couldn't manage to make out the sound of her breathing.

He left the packet of sweets on a chair, the paper crackling slightly as it settled against the furniture, and without even taking off his hat, he sat on the edge of the easy chair at the foot of the marriage bed. There he fixed his gaze on the brightness of the little lamp, which behind the jug of water appeared as a fan of light.

The alternating rhythm of his children's breathing, as they slept peacefully, came to his ears. A golden spark did crazy turns inside the lamp, then suddenly disappeared: some little butterfly, perhaps, which had ended by scorching itself in the flame.

As Daniel's eyes fixed on the point where the yellow brilliance emerged, with a halo forming where the beams of luminous needles advanced and drew back, his vision diminished and began to quaver. At the same time, he had the sensation a merciful irrigation was passing over the dryness of his soul. The tears came at last, ones that sprang up wildly and proudly, without any vulgar gesture or squinting of the eyes to stem their flow.

At that moment he understood he'd begun a new life . . .

Summer Sun

Stolen waters are sweet
and bread eaten in secret is pleasant.
SOLOMON
Proverbs, Chapter 9 verse 7

As he entered, Samuel noticed that the doors leading off from the hallway were closed. To observe this was enough for his mind to yet again develop the plan so many times built up and so many times ruined by insignificant circumstance.

In the sewing room, three ladies sat completely absorbed in their work.

They smiled at him in welcome, used to considering him a member of the family, and Julia, the girl, pulled over a low chair, his favorite.

Summer began to heat up the city. The air was stifling and drained their energy.

Doña Clarisa yawned, throwing her head back and resting her hands on her thighs; Maria yawned, looking at Samuel out of the corner of her eye and putting a hand over her mouth; Julia yawned, turning the end of her yawn into a song. Discreetly, Samuel yawned too. They looked at each other and laughed, and slowly a conversation emerged, idle, torpid.

"Are you heading to the coast this year?"

"Yes, almost certainly. It's so good for the children."

"Lucky you. We plan to spend the summer in Santiago," said María, not lifting her eyes from her work.

"The holidays can be amusing here," Samuel replied, lighting a cigarette. "If it weren't for Elisa and the children, I'd prefer not to leave Santiago either."

He met the eyes of María, who gave him a smile of disbelief.

That woman brought him a special kind of happiness. Without a doubt she wasn't a beauty; she had a big mouth and snub nose, and her skin was sprinkled with freckles. But that big mouth had a delectable charm, and when it opened it showed the fresh whiteness of perfect teeth; that small nose gave her features a certain wonderful picaresque air; and that complexion sown with freckles had a smooth and truly charming softness. Then there were María's eyes, big and black, with light circles beneath them as in women of the East. Despite being married and a mother, her body was still harmonious in its lines and flexible in its movements, like the body of a young single woman. The only place the consequence of maternity was noticeable was at her bust, wide, powerful, which filled her bodice so that it had no fold or wrinkle.

Samuel had come to that house for the first time a little over a year before, as a neighborly visit. At the start they'd kept their relations within the bounds of a stiff, indifferent courtesy. Both families practiced the social game of visits received and repaid, until attracted by María's slow seduction, he'd ended up sharing his life with these kind people.

In this way, through calm hours spent in intimacy, there had developed in him, without him realizing it, the affection he now felt for a woman who'd once left him frozen with her modesty of a great lady, and who later, without giving Samuel any reason to change his respectful idea of her, came to awaken hopes in his spirit and even desires for love.

The conversation wound on, pleasant, cheerful. Doña Clarisa, wearing glasses that slipped toward the tip of her nose, leaning over her work and raising her head at times to peep over the lenses, recalled in an interminable monologue those times when the whole family, summer after summer, had made the trip by car to Cartagena.

Samuel heard Doña Clarisa's voice without understanding what it was saying, just as one hears a faraway murmur. All his attention was fixed on María, who at that moment was undoing the stitches of a seam and bringing the threads to her mouth, keeping them as prisoners between her lips.

With what infinite tenderness he looked at those full lips, moving slightly, continuously moistened by a quick flick of the tongue . . .

The heat of the patio bathed in sun passed through the overheated wooden door. Doña Clarisa yawned again, and everyone did the same. Then they all laughed, glancing at each other.

"My God, Mama, you're going to infect us with your laziness . . ." exclaimed María, stretching in a way that drew attention to her bust, and crossing one leg over the other in her chair.

Her skirt bunched up when she made this movement, and left a well-shaped leg exposed, the exquisite shape of which stood out in its tight black stocking.

Samuel stood up and said he was going. He put on his jacket and gave a reluctant smile.

"Where could you be going in this heat?"

Hat in hand, without taking a step, a little embarrassed and awkward, Samuel insisted he had to leave.

"I have to do something downtown . . . at three."

He took out his watch. María looked at hers, which she wore fastened to her bodice.

"You're going to melt in the street. Sit down, stay a while longer."

Without taking off his hat, Samuel sat again.

Now he didn't know what to talk about. But María eased the way for him, asking if he'd gone to the theater.

As a matter of fact, the night before he'd been at the "Santiago", at the premiere of *The Count of Luxembourg* by an Italian operetta company.

He started to praise the music in the work, without daring to recount the plot.

"And were there many people in the audience?"

It was the only thing that interested Julia. For her, a lovely outing didn't exist unless it involved many people. Samuel found himself obliged to make great efforts of memory and recall some of the families in attendance at the performance.

"The Errázuriz family was there . . . the Ovalles . . . the Izquierdos . . . the Fabres . . ."

"And the Claros?"

"No. The Claros, no. The Fernándezes were there . . . the Tagles . . ."

He couldn't satisfy Julia about the dresses the girls wore, because he hadn't noticed them.

María's skirt was still gathered up, and the vision of her well-shaped leg disturbed him, filling him with confusion. He thought of the plan he'd developed as he came in. If when saying goodbye, María accompanied him to the exit as she always did, and they passed through the dark entrance hall . . .

He stood up again, resolved.

"I pity you . . . In this heat . . ." said Doña Clarisa, as she saw him approach her.

And then, after giving him her hand:

"But you aren't hot. Your hand is cool, almost frozen."

Samuel murmured some words, laughed exaggeratedly, and then went out, preceded by María.

"There's so much sun on the patio it would be better to go through here," she told him, gesturing with her eyes toward a door.

They passed through dark, fresh rooms where golden light filtered through the shutters.

Samuel didn't know where he was going. He felt something unpleasant in his stomach, and damp ice in his hands. He tried to walk faster, wanted to reach María but couldn't. With astonishing quickness of mind he imagined the fatal or happy consequences of what he was about to do. He searched for previous cases on which to ground a decision. He remembered a time his hand had brushed against hers, and she hadn't drawn it away, hadn't even shown annoyance. In an instant his mind produced a sum of all the gazes, all the smiles, all the words by María that might contain affection for him.

All at once, his imagination stopped; his thought went blank.

They'd arrived at the entrance hall. María gave a turn, then another, to the key in the door that led to the hallway. It was the decisive moment.

He said something. And she too answered something, something he didn't understand, didn't hear. He saw only the smile on her lips, a languid, drooping smile that seemed to call to him. At that moment he felt himself grow faint, as if his being were dissolving into María. He moved forward, pupils dilated, not seeing anything around him, and just when his spirits were faltering most, a soothing ripple moved through his entire body. Her arms, plump, smooth, rose up and slid themselves around his neck, a warm perfume surrounded him, and against his chest he could feel the pressure, the soft firmness, of that longed-for bust . . . Then, forgetting everything, he grabbed her by the waist and kissed her lips for a long time.

Then he flung himself into the street blazing with sun, carrying in his brain the shadows of the entrance hall, and within those shadows the vision of that passionate woman, smiling, overcome at last, eyes dark, breast agitated, all love and all tenderness, in the unforgettable pose in which he'd seen her as he made his exit.

The Defense

> . . . and love, to my understanding, is giving,
> or at least its essence resides in the desire
> to do good or give happiness . . .[1]
>
> RUSKIN
> *Modern Painters*

I

Have I been a villain? It's so easy to judge the actions of others, like this, at a distance, without examining the causes that determined them! What a simple mental operation it is to say: this one is a thief because he robbed, that

---

1 The Spanish phrasing is a loose version of the original, which reads: ". . . for love, I think, chiefly grows in giving, at least its essence is the desire of doing good, or giving happiness . . ." Magallanes Moure's version of *Los pintores modernos* was likely the one translated by the Spanish writer Carmen de Burgos (Valencia Prometeo, 1913).

one is a cheat because he lied, the other is a murderer because he killed. Ah! If judges had the perception necessary to understand the state of criminals' souls at the moment they committed their crimes, what a mad oscillation their judgment would experience before they passed any sentence, how unpleasantly their hand would sway before they signed an order!

There are occasions on which one steals and is not a thief, one kills and is not a murderer . . .

Ours might have been a crime, but for God's sake, my friend, neither she nor I are criminals. We have struggled against evil so far as we've been able: she, asking for help from God; me, clinging to duty. We've resisted the entreaties of the constant and powerful voice that called to us both, that told us to enter the desired place, to go in, since we'd be alone there, protected by generous shadow . . . We've ignored that voice for as long as we could, for as long as it didn't transform into an imperative and irresistible command.

You don't know all the agonies, all the tortures, all the tribulations that have lacerated my soul in the battle unleashed against temptation!

You say I've been a villain because I, a married man, fell in love with a woman who was also married, and we didn't know how to rein back this passion which God and law condemn. How easy it is to say all this! How simple it is, my friend, to judge the actions others commit! And how difficult, how horribly difficult it is to be truly just toward others!

II

I don't need to repeat to you my ideas about morals and duty. You know me, you know I'm an honorable man, and that's enough. It pains me, however, that you haven't asked me, before casting an anathema upon me, the causes by which I, the honorable and austere man that you've known, have transformed into what you call a villain.

My life was calm, so calm! Free of great aspirations, friend to order and repose, my happiness was enclosed in this little house, no larger than my ambition. In love with my wife, with the kind-hearted Matilde whom I never stopped loving, happy with my children, whose character is a reflection of the sweet character of their mother, I lived without cares or ambitions, alternating the quiet pleasures of the home with the satisfactions of diligent, well-paid work. It was the ideal life, the life dreamed of during my time as a studious, meditative young man. Love, joy and peace, great peace . . .

Nevertheless . . . take note of the way that with such calm, such gentleness, tragedy descends upon us.

One day, from that very window there, facing the table where I'm writing to you, I noticed a great bustle in the house at the corner, a house with nothing extraordinary about it, identical to many houses in Santiago. It had remained uninhabited, with a "to let" sign for several months, and now, the most natural thing in the world, vehicles were coming to it loaded with furniture, the sign we had new neighbors.

Who were these new neighbors?

What happened outside my home had never interested me, and without feeling the slightest curiosity as to what I'd seen, I went back to my table and buried myself in the plans for a construction project I wanted to get done soon.

That same day at dinner, Matilde said to me:

"Do you know people have moved into the house on the corner?"

"Ah, yes . . ." I said, thinking of something else. "Today I saw they brought furniture."

"But you don't know what family it might be?"

I made a gesture and smiled, letting her understand there was no way I could know, not having left the house all afternoon. Matilde saw I had nothing to contribute, and we spoke about other things.

Two days later, at lunch, my wife let me know the family on the corner was known by hers.

"They're very good people," she added, "distinguished and wealthy, and I think we should make a neighborhood visit as soon as possible. Sunday . . . what do you say?"

Even though I don't consider myself to be a cynical man—and even less so then—something in me blindly resists meeting new people. Matilde, who knew this, made an effort to convince me this way of thinking was flawed.

"Life in society is necessary," she repeated to me, every time the occasion arose. "Isolation leads to illness in men like you, who work all day long. One has to go out, distract oneself, talk with people who aren't the same as those we see every day, exchange ideas . . ."

Life in society . . . How to confess to her my ideas about that false and complex life, full of labyrinths and crossroads, like a hostile land?

How to make her share a distrust of mine that was perhaps no more than prejudice?

So I agreed, although reluctantly, and we went for that stiff and formal visit.

The family was composed of five people: the mistress of the house—a respectable widow whose graying head invited one to remember other times and restore with the imagination a beauty whose elements, somewhat faded by the years, were still there in a sweet noble face—along with her married daughter, sad and lovely, and her husband—a very healthy, smart-looking gentleman, whose conversation served us that afternoon as an aperitif, for he spoke to us of the exquisite foods lately rustled up by the Club's *maître*, which he described in picturesque language, giving us a triple sensation of their color, smell and flavor. In addition, there were two chattering and laughing girls, who moved about in their chairs as if wishing for the visit to be quickly over. Ah! and two boys, the sons of the married woman.

The married woman! Poor lady, so good, so beautiful, and joined to that man in whose spirit every form of cruelty seemed to have made its home, every form of coarseness . . .

III

My construction project was finished. To draw up the budget of expenses, an operation at which I wasn't very skilled, as I wasn't up-to-date on the value of materials, I had to consult a friend, an employee at the Public Works Department.

We'd work at his office from four to five, and then I'd go home to take advantage of the last hours of the day to tidy my accounts.

Every afternoon, therefore, I passed before her house.

I say "her", and the simple word fills my soul with tenderness.

Every afternoon she was at the window, behind the glass, looking with a distracted gaze at the comings and goings of passersby, pale, serene, with a light shadow in the expression of her noble face.

One night I was working hard to finish an urgent job, I heard voices in the living room, which is the room beneath my study. Then the servant came to tell me that the family on the corner was in my home, making a visit. At first, the event irritated me. I needed to finish the job and wasn't in a situation to put it down, and go exchange greetings and courtesies downstairs. But my wife came up and in a voice choked with haste begged me to be polite to her friends. I was forced to agree. In the living room were Mama, "she" and one of the girls. When I entered, the lady and girl spoke as a pair with my wife. Then "she" turned her admirable eyes toward me and smiled.

Was it that look? That smile?

No, no. Our love was not the sudden and fatal love of stories. And if that night she'd looked at me and smiled with love . . . it's certain I wouldn't have been infatuated. My idea of duty would have prevented me.

It was neither that night, nor the following, nor . . . Oh, I couldn't say when! It was that night, and the next, and the next, all the nights we were together, all the nights we spoke to one another, smiled at one another, looked at one another, were silent with one another . . . Over the course of all those nights, and then over the course of all those days, our love formed, grew, developed.

In this way, too, over many nights and many days, the bud of a plant forms, grows and develops, until there comes a little ray of sun, a stray breeze or light push of sap, and the bud becomes a flower. In the same way my sleeping love flourished, in a moment, in a second, in a lightning bolt of time.

Do not think that if I prolong myself in these details it is to strengthen my defense, which is, ay!, our defense.

Villainy, what you call villainy, has not been ours; what has been ours is life, because life, life alone, determined to throw us into each other's arms.

Soon the cold atmosphere surrounding us went about warming. We started to get to know each other. In her conversations, very delicate and also very simple, Irene let me glimpse more than once the sadness of her life beside that man who didn't understand her, didn't respect her; who no longer felt even admiration for her beauty. He was a practical man, absolutely deprived of sensibility, deprived of all emotion that wasn't about making a good deal in the stock market, always worried about supply and demand, with no aspiration but to make a lot of money. One of those men, in short, who like the brute Esau, are capable of selling, I won't say birthright, but even honor, even what they once loved, for a fistful of ninepence banknotes . . .

Little by little the friendship went weaving subtle nets around Irene and me, the kind whose power of resistance is only noticed at the moment one wishes to break them.

Everyone at Irene's house got on well with me, all flattered me, all showed me affection. I became one more in the family. Doña Carmen asked me for advice about the administration of her assets; the girls happily submitted their flirtations to my consideration; Carlos, that scoundrel, imposed on me all the news referring to his business and his adventures; and the little ones brought me their dolls so I could fit an arm or leg back into place, sometimes a head. Even the cat Michín came up to me, and arching his back, pricking up his shuddering tail, he rubbed his glossy black fur against my leg, at the same time he opened and closed his big green eyes in slow voluptuous blinking.

How could I foresee the consequences of such intimacy? How easy it is, from the heights, to trace the direction of a path! I, who moved along it, couldn't take in its constant winding, much less realize the place to which it was leading.

By the time I noticed the danger, it was too late to dispel it . . .

My wife, who always joked with me about Irene—when referring to her beauty she never stopped repeating "careful!"—entered my study one day, and feigning an expression of tranquility, to which the grave tone in her voice gave the lie, told me it was necessary for me to distance my visits to Irene's house, since in the neighborhood whispers were beginning to be heard about our friendship.

Sure of my freedom of spirit, I wanted to make a display of it.

"Do you mean to say they think I'm in love with Irene?"

Matilde didn't dare to answer, maybe afraid to upset me.

"Nothing could be simpler," I went on. "I won't go to that house anymore. It will all be over."

The simplicity of resolutions like this, at first intention!

You must believe me if I say that after the conclusive declaration made to my wife, I went back to burying myself in my work with the greatest calm in the world. But now I suspect that at the very moment I expressed to my wife what I'm telling you, something began to germinate in the darkest part of my soul, like a seed in the damp underground. In speaking to her, I began to suspect the truth that I was deceiving myself when I announced I wouldn't return to Irene's house, the truth that nothing or no one could separate us anymore. But I swear to you I was resolved then to keep the promise that Matilde heard from me.

IV

I kept it for a period of many days, during which I passed again and again before Irene's window, greeting her as usual with a long look and friendly smile.

At the start she answered my greetings pleasantly, and returned the looks and smiles. But as time went on, and I didn't go see her, her expression changed to become grave and sad, as before.

One afternoon, coming back from downtown, I saw her go out to the balcony at the same moment I passed her house. She was serious and rather pale. She didn't answer my greeting, but called out to me with a somewhat urgent gesture.

Resting her bust between her crossed arms, on the balcony's ledge, she turned her head in my direction to speak with me:

"Sorry if I'm bothering you but I've waited for so many days, and I think you've forgotten my request . . ."

She smiled with melancholy as she spoke.

Her words confused me, since I didn't understand what the request might be.

I strained my memory, and nothing, not the slightest recollection. Meanwhile, she kept looking at me, smiling with sadness.

"You've forgotten, isn't that right? And now that a good book to distract myself in the evening is so necessary . . . Now that I have to stay up all night . . ."

Then I remembered that a long time before, a very long time, I'd offered her *The Lily in the Valley*, a poignant novel by Balzac.

"Excuse me, ma'am, I've been so busy these days . . ."

"More than me? Just imagine, I have Carlitos sick, with a fever and a cough. It seems to be pneumonia."

She spoke in anguished tones. She told me about her boy's illness, asked me for advice, and when I made a gesture to say goodbye, she held me back with these words.

"The saddest thing for me is finding myself alone . . ."

"But your Mama, the girls . . ." I replied.

"Ah! That's true," she exclaimed with a sigh.

When I got home, I told Matilde about the boy's illness. The news affected her. I had to tell her all the details Irene had given me.

My wife repeated at every moment:

"How upset she must be! . . . Poor Irene! Poor Irene!"

After dinner, once she'd put the children to bed, Matilde climbed upstairs to my study to suggest we go check on Carlitos.

Before I could open my mouth to answer, she stacked up reasons upon arguments to persuade me that we should go. The pathos of her phrases convinced me, and I concluded by sighing, I too truly moved:

"Poor Irene . . . Poor Irene . . ."

V

Carlos, the father, wasn't home. He hadn't even eaten there.

Matilde entered the boy's room where Irene was, and I stayed in the sitting room with Doña Carmen and one of the girls. I observed all the consternation that a serious illness brings to an affectionate home. People went about on tiptoe, spoke in low voices, wore expressions alert to the echo of a sound or someone's appearance. The good lady rested her white head on her chest, and interlacing her hands on her skirt, repeated between sighs:

"Poor Irene . . . Poor Irene . . ."

And Raquel, the happy girl with the eternal laugh, whispered so seriously she didn't seem to be herself:

"Poor Irene!"

Poor Irene, I said to myself too, in the depths of my soul. Poor mother, poor woman, so good, so beautiful, so sad and so miserable! A sweet gentleness spilled forth within me; an almost voluptuous wave of tenderness bathed my nerves, which became delicate, sensitive to the point of spasm. Poor Irene! Then my soul was taken up by the whirlwind of an idea that elevated me above all the meanness of the world, and with all my strength of mind, I asked myself: "Who could make her happy?"

The next day I passed by in the morning to find out about the sick boy. His conditioned remained grave. I didn't see Irene.

I came back in the afternoon. At the door I met Carlos, who was going out, hat tilted back, hands in trouser pockets, a Havana cigar between his teeth whose thread of smoke made him squint one eye. I asked after the boy.

"He's getting better, getting better."

And taking out a hand weighed down with rings, he plucked the cigar from his mouth:

"Women get jumpy about everything and alarm everyone. There they are, all depressed. You go in, go in . . ."

I don't know why the idea of entering, invited by him, gave me such repulsion, and I preferred to avoid it.

That evening, I went with Matilde. It was true there'd been a favorable reaction in the sick boy, but not so decisive as to drive away the terrible concern.

At the request of Doña Carmen, I entered the boy's bedroom for a moment.

The lamp on the dresser spread a pale clarity throughout the room, dim as the spectral light that illuminates our dreams. Before I could move forward, the figure of Irene emerged before me. Instinctively I looked for her hand, which joined with mine in a long clasp. I felt a pleasure as vivid, as sharp, as that produced by the most maddening caress. As in a haze, the pale smudge of her face in darkness, with the circular shadows of her eyes and the dark shadow of her mouth, grew brighter and faded before my eyes. Then our hands released one another and I was left trembling, disoriented, the palpitations of my confused beating heart booming in my head.

VI

After that . . .

I could finish here, my friend, sure the impulse that made you condemn me, condemn us, will by now have turned to pity. But I'll go

82

on with this confession that will perhaps succeed in modifying your inflexible judgment of a moral theorist.

After that . . .

Now that the sick boy was out of danger, the oppressive anguish of before was replaced with a joy edging on bliss. The nerves slackened and eased in the calm elation of a tranquility achieved at last.

I continued to visit Irene's house at all hours, sometimes with Matilde, other times alone, and each time I was received with more affection, more delight. And when through an excess of work I spent a day without going, Doña Carmen told me without the others hearing:

"Why didn't you come yesterday? You're the only one who knows how to distract Irene, make her happy . . ."

I made great efforts to dissuade the good lady from her idea, but the insistence with which she replied gave me great pleasure:

"What I tell you is true. Ah! if instead of having married that man, who's so . . ."

She didn't finish the sentence. There was no need. Everything had been said.

Then Irene appeared, smiling, with the languidness of those beings intoxicated with just a bit of happiness, like those people who never drink alcohol and feel they're in paradise after a few sips.

Irene appeared, more beautiful now she suffered less, her thick brown hair swept to one side—it was, as she well knew, the style that best pleased me—her delicious body molded by her simple and elegant house dress, all of her fresh, all of her fragrant as a flower.

She arrived, surrendered her hand to the prolonged pressure of mine, and sat down facing me. That way we could talk and look at one another as much as we liked.

Sometimes restless Raquel or excitable Erna made jokes about us:

"Look at them, Erna, they're such good friends."

"Ah, yes! They understand each other so wonderfully well."

"As if they were . . . My God! I was about to say something awful!" said Raquel, letting out a sharp cackle.

"How silly the girls are!" said Irene, her face full of joy.

Once Erna referred to us as sweethearts, and Irene became serious and fell into a melancholy meditation that made tears spring to her eyes. Bringing her hand to her face, she got up and left the room without a word. We remained in silence. The girls blamed each other in turn for what had happened.

"You know she gets nervous . . ."

"And you . . ."

"I'm not as annoying as you are."

"But you tease her a lot, too."

They went out in search of her, but came back alone.

"She's with the boy."

"She says she's coming . . ."

And when the hour came to say goodbye, she didn't appear.

"Poor Irene!" I thought, over and over. "Who could make her happy!"

Ah! This idea that I could bring that tired, sad life a bit of relief, maybe a bit of happiness; this idea that everyone made a great effort to cultivate in me, until it took root; this idea, which so exactly corresponds to the impulse that makes us pour fresh water on a plant drooping from thirst, sharing with our imagination in some of the plant's pleasure when it receives the irrigation; this idea was the cause of my tragedy, our tragedy.

I attempted to cheer up that melancholy life; I dreamed, madness of mine!, to make a happy creature of that beautiful sad woman; I had the illusion, the gorgeous illusion, that my love, like a ray of sun in winter, could make her sorrow and bitterness evaporate . . .

VII

For the rest, let me say nothing. We were happy . . .

For how long? I don't know, I don't know. Those days of happiness are so far away, so high above. They seem like tiny stars viewed from the depth of a well!

Omnia transit. Isn't that your motto?

Yes, everything passes, everything!

But sometimes, in my prolonged escapes to the land of dream, as the rest chatter and laugh around me, the beloved idea sprouts within my soul, grows, gives out flowers like before:

"Poor Irene . . . Who could make her happy? She deserves it so much! So much!"

So, What is It?

What is Love. There is no question mark in the title of Manuel Magallanes Moure's collection. No reply is expected. As with Lenin's *What is to be Done?* (which does have a question mark, but nevertheless reads as a statement, since the essay tries to give a clear answer to the question), the phrase's spareness has an unsettling quality. The defamiliarizing string of words becomes a threshold to new ideas, new sensations.

At the risk of glibness, it occurs to me that the title of Magallanes Moure's book can be read literally. *What* is love, with "whatness" an undefined quality, a kind of absurdity beyond reason.

But let me try again. "Love" is always "to love", a dialogue or conversation, something active that requires (at least) two, just like writing, reading, translating. And those two (or more) might be people, or might not.

To love is to translate constantly—words and gestures are never innocent, but arrive packed with meanings, in hermetic form. The simplicity that one desires comes from a kind of attention, a focus on certain elements within the vast zone of interpretation. Perhaps love requires an understanding that attention also requires a sacrifice of comprehension, an acknowledgement that there is much one does not know that makes the other a separate consciousness. Beyond the bounds of the individual self, beyond knowledge, there is rich mystery. To translate that richness into understanding, and into a dialogue with the known, requires the translator's every resource and changes her in the process. (Just as she, in turn, affects the other.)

To write is to translate constantly—the object is changed into words. I could tell this as a parable. A writer saw a tram speed by, and instead of describing its speed and power, he wrote "tram." His work became stoic and minimal, and at first he believed the world of nouns was more direct and pure. But after some time writing this way, he sensed that tram was a mere word. He tried not to impose his ideas of tramness onto it, but let it be what it wanted. He became comprehensive and receptive: a mystic. The sensory data that came to him ceased to be processed by his mind. Yet love, even of words, requires one to reach out toward the other. The noun needs deciphering to become a verb, to live. And so the writer's book went to press with a tram thrumming from emotion, as understood by the narrator.

This is a thought exercise. I don't know if the author of the book here had any such ideas. But he does view his objects with sentiment. To find human emotion in inanimate things is a sentimental fallacy, says the critic. If you attribute emotion to nature, as with a powerful mountain or meditative river, you're actually referring to the emotion of the one who's viewing them. The same goes for a throwaway remark or a way of folding the hands. Even those who try to simply describe a table (the Robbe-Grillets of the world) inevitably bring perception into it. So why not make the connection explicit? Magallanes Moure translates the things of the world not fixed as symbols, but subject to change, deterioration, ambiguity, and doubt, to alteration and new development. The speeding tram, the shadow moving over the wall, the ticking clock, the printing press in action—even the swirl of music—all are in movement, and Magallanes Moure takes them up and bestows them with his and his narrators' emotions.

To read is to translate constantly—the word is brought back into the world, and renewed perception is given to objects. One seeks not to illuminate things, but to be illuminated by them. The reader might emerge from stories with a new readiness to participate, equipped with a new vocabulary for how to read things and situations, which she combines with other vocabularies, or discards, or takes up to invent a grammar of her own, completing the circle by becoming a writer. (Of course, none of that might happen either, with the moment of reading existing for its own sake.)

To translate is to translate constantly—I know that sounds tautological. If so, it's because out of these three enigmatic figures (the writer, the translator, the reader), it's the translator who lacks contact with the object itself. She doesn't interpret the thing (as the writer does) or approach the thing with a new interpretation (the reader), but shuttles between interpretations in an atmosphere of pure words. A hell of logos. In what way can she find the mystery of the beloved object again? Where can she rediscover the world? One answer is to embrace the other roles of writer and reader, to become a lover of language and the world. To translate is also to be translated into other roles. Another answer is that through the translation itself, she can keep the referent moving, unsettling the language and message, making the words as active as the tram, clock, shadows, printing press, music.

And now I'll repeat myself.

To love is to translate constantly.

"How can Love be explained? The intellect attempting to convey it is like an ass in the morass, and the pen that is to describe it breaks into pieces," writes Annemarie Schimmel in *Rumi's World: The Life and Works of the Greatest Sufi Poet*. Magallanes Moure doesn't so much answer the question as change it to a different one—*how is love?*

In these four stories, the Chilean writer introduces subtle new forms of affection, all of which lie outside the traditional Catholic model of heterosexual marriage and ultimately are rendered impossible by the society of his time.

He wrote these stories while he himself was married, to all descriptions happily and with a child. In this sense, his tales are not so much a call for the rupture of this arrangement as they are an evocation of the temptations, moments of anguish, niggling doubts, and flirtations (or beyond) that can exist within its framework, adding layers of complexity to its foundation. The characters are not brave or cruel enough to truly break with their circumstances; instead, they observe their surroundings, carefully note their inner worlds, and struggle to make compromises.

In his time, Magallanes Moure was principally known as a poet rather than as a writer of stories, although his initial studies were in art. At the Escuela de Bellas Artes, one of his teachers was Pedro Lira, one of Chile's best known artists. Although Lira is most famous for his historical painting *The Foundation of Santiago*, the majority of his work shows countrysides and interiors where light and shade play off one another to create suggestive spaces, with secret alcoves of quietude or repose. Lira's scenes generally express not so much action as mood: the transition between parts of a day, or between fleeting contemplations by a solitary individual. In his work, one can appreciate the blending of muted colors, the subtle shifts of tone, the concentration of seriousness and melancholy into a single figure, the folds of garments, the play of light: in short, the creation of sensual atmospheres.

Looking at the images that Magallanes Moure created, one notes that he learned a great deal from this style. His landscapes adopt similar elements, even if they lack the dexterity, and perhaps the confidence, of his teacher. Magallanes Moure contributed illustrations to magazines, such as one that shows the French writer Jules Barbey D'Aurevilly, that explorer of hidden motivations in the aristocratic classes. The image captures his self-conscious, dandyish romanticism through an arched eyebrow, long combed hair, a groomed mustache, an elaborate lapelled coat, and a hand on the hip. Another, showing the Russian writer Maxim Gorki—a realist with an interest in portraying the effects of social pressures on individual men's lives— depicts a furrowed brow and pained expression. It's hard not to read these portraits of anguished intellectuals as, at least to some extent, spiritual renderings of Magallanes Moure's state of mind. A picture of Magallanes Moure himself exists, made by his teacher Pedro Lira, in which the attributes are similar: an aristocratic suit, a combed yet stylishly disheveled mop of hair, eyes lost somewhere far away.

Magallanes Moure would also write art criticism for *El Mercurio*, where his work appeared under the pseudonym "M. de Ávila", as well as journalism for publications like *Las Últimas Noticias*; he also edited the magazines *Pluma y Lápiz* and *Chile Ilustrado* in Santiago, and would later found the newspaper *La Reforma* in San Bernardo. His poems began to appear in magazines like *Zig Zag* and *Juventud*, as well as in published volumes. In the controversial anthology of the period *Selva Lírica*, famous for its highly opinionated, toe-treading descriptions of well-known contemporary poets within the sensitive milieu of early 20th century Chilean literature, the compilers Julio Molina Nuñez and Juan Agustin Araya show themselves to be a bit skeptical of Magallanes Moure's early works *Facetas* (1902) and *Matices* (1904), which they claim, identifying the works with the man himself, "represent the period of his evolution from romanticism to modernism: certain ideas half-drawn from lyrical relics are submitted to a frame of young flesh and dressed up in glossy modern clothing, to give a manly appearance of placid rebellion." In *La Jornada* (1910), in contrast, Magallanes Moure sings to "all that sweeps him toward the imperious need to quiver with varied sensations, experienced at the precise blue hour of psychic tension." They continue, in their overwrought prose: "To date we have found no poet who makes of Love such a healthy, mystic, salutary, emotional philosophy as Magallanes. His verses seem to be inspired by the heat of an eastern lamp, beneath the trembling pink softness of rosy twilight." In style they compare his poetry to that of Eduardo Marquina, Francisco Villaespesa, Juan Ramón Jiménez, and Amado Nervo.

Although these anthologists represent Magallanes Moure at his most able as an art critic, they also note his incursions into other forms, giving special attention to his plays *El pecado bendito* and *La batalla*, and the stories in this collection: "In 1914 we are presented with a delicate philosopher, an incorruptible stylist, who pours his refined artistic temperament into the pages of *Qué es amor* (What is Love), a collection of beautiful stories that includes 'Sol de estío' (Summer Sun), which took first prize in *El Mercurio*'s 1913 contest."

To my mind, the stories of *Qué es amor*, although delicate and stylish to be sure, mark a shift from Magallanes Moure's previous work, and break precisely with his image of love as healthy or mystical, as attributed to him by Nuñez and Araya. The stories' deceptive simplicity presents a far more ambiguous vignette about the small daily tortures and resignations of a mind conflicted between the regularity of bourgeois happiness, and the promises of a life fully dedicated to art in a freer, looser, more open existence. The equivalent of Magallanes Moure's impressionistic visual artworks, these stories offer a landscape of the emotions. The bourgeois chooses the peace of regularity, but suffers as he intuits other possibilities, in glinting moments of real joy.

To understand the change in Magallanes Moure's philosophy, perhaps one can take into account his vital experiences between the early poetic work of *Facetas* and *Matices*, and the later work of *La jornada* and *Qué es amor*. During the period from 1904-1905, which these anthologizers represent in their portrait as a shift in Magallanes Moure's trajectory, he lived through various significant episodes. One of these involved his loan of a plot of land in rural San Bernardo to the founding members of an attempted Tolstoyan Colony, the writers Fernando Santiván, Augusto D'Halmar and Julio Ortiz de Zárate. The attempted commune fizzled out from a lack of logistics, internal differences, sexual tensions between the men, and urban misunderstanding of what farming work in the countryside truly involves. The members of the group, however, remained artistic brothers. And in many ways, this might be considered an early project of Los Diez, one of the most renowned Chilean cultural groups of the 20th century.

Los Diez was a fluid, shifting set of friends—including Magallanes Moure and these members of the Tolstoyan colony—who came together to mingle different art forms, and who, within the neocolonial house they chose as their headquarters, encouraged an atmosphere of high playfulness. For two years (1916-1917), the group published books as well as a literary magazine, but its activities extended before and after this in chronology and scope—from architectural plans to alter the house (today a historical monument, the "Casa de Los Diez"), to silly rituals encouraging friendship that involved alcohol, ceremonies and costumes, to the writing of manifestos and other texts. At heart, "Los Diez" was a spontaneous exchange by like-minded souls without any grand over-arching philosophical ideas, but with a basic and near-holy impulse to create art, question convention, and build an atmosphere of camaraderie. More than any "thing in itself," the group treasured the forms of beauty that could derive from fellowship in creation.

Jean Emar, writing in *La Nacion* in 1924 about an art exhibition featuring Magallanes Moure's work, offered a good description of the group along the way:

> The poet, like many of those who made their weapons artistic ones, enjoyed creating with verses, splotches, jottings, even easel paintings. That whole generation, which at one time was united as a faithful, compact group, "Los Diez", was possessed of a broad, youthful, artistic eclecticism. The poets painted, the writers painted, the architects and sculptors painted. The bond that so strongly held together all for the benefit of all was crystallized in painting. This tie was artistic fraternity, and support amongst those who nourished the same aesthetic ideals.

A decade went by, but in 1914, the year *Qué es amor* was published, Magallanes Moure was still engaged in creative work. He had a rich inner life. He also kept up correspondences with several people, most notably Gabriela Mistral and Pedro Prado, poets with whom he had close and complex friendships. Let's start with the second. To Prado, a fellow member of Los Diez, he wrote letters that communicate something of his desire and anguish at that time. At the time Prado was trying to get him to edit a magazine called *Chile Contemporáneo*, which they decided they'd simply call *Chile*. While Magallanes Moure was intrigued by the potential literary project, his mind was taken up by other matters as well, and through letters one can trace a shift in his psyche. For example, on January 22, 1914, he writes:

> I spent all day outside at Playa Ancha, with my wife and daughter (. . .) Everything is lovely, even the bars. And the women . . . so healthy, so happy, so simple. I imagine them clean underneath, sweet-smelling, firm. I'd like to be a friend to all of them, and not

want to love any of them. I'd like to chatter away with them. But don't be alarmed: I already know where these innocent desires might lead. "Life's a sly devil." Isn't that so?

On February 8, he sends Prado a more domestic note from Cartagena, in Valparaíso. His wife is getting over an illness, and he is with her and his daughter:

Don't pay any attention to the tired and drowsy tone of my words: it's noon, it's Sunday, and I'm sleepy. I went to the post office after lunch and they didn't give me a thing. But I took advantage of the outing to buy a cigar, and I'm smoking it, not so much at ease as I'd like because it's insisted on burning unevenly. I'm in my room, which is also that of my wife and Mireya (. . .) Oh soft white bed, so silently inviting at the time for rest, on your affectionate lap man discovers life

and death, love and dream . . .
and sometimes cruel fleas or vile
bedbugs!

That same year, Magallanes Moure was a judge
of the Juegos Florales literary prize awarded
to Gabriela Mistral for her *Sonnets of Death*,
a work of Catholic imagery shot through by
theosophy that introduces her idea of the res-
urrection of the flesh. In it, pain, languor and
silence, seemingly unromantic ideas, come to
bear a heavy sensual weight. Mistral famously
declined to receive the prize in person because
she didn't want to stand before a crowd with a
wreath of flowers on her head. That same year,
the two struck up a complicated friendship that
would last for decades, but centered around a
period of nine years (1914-1923). Their intense, emotional letters cover a wide variety of
topics from metaphysics to gossip about contemporaries' literary production, but is most
of all about longing—phrased in very earthly
expressions of bodily desire. Mistral writes of
yearning for Magallanes Moure's lips, dream-
ing of mystical union, taking the drug ether to
feel herself in a gentle dream state, and wanting
to "drink down all your lymph."

The two kindled their special relationship despite an eleven year age gap, the fact he had a wife and daughter, and differing class backgrounds. She was a rural schoolteacher and still unrecognized poet—it would have shocked those around her to be told she'd win the Nobel Prize in Literature in 1945; she took on grueling and underpaid work in the south of Chile, in the cities of Los Andes, Punta Arenas, and Temuco, with a painful experience of death behind her. (A former lover, the railworker Romelio Ureta, had committed suicide.) Although passionate, she was unsure of herself, and still wrote as Lucila Godoy, not Gabriela Mistral. Meanwhile, Magallanes Moure was a gentleman of letters who moved between Santiago, San Bernardo and El Melocotón, surrounded by his artistic group and established in the capital city's bourgeois literary world. Yet the fact he wrote *Qué es amor*, a book so full of subtle longing and frustration, the year he began his correspondence with Mistral speaks to his unstable emotional state.

The two writers had to take care to be discreet, since Mistral's correspondence was looked on with suspicion at her local post office, where she'd requested the letters be sent, rather than to her home or school. For his part, Magallanes

Moure had to conceal the correspondence from his family. The Chile of the time, then as now, was a very small world. Yet the two regularly managed to send each other books and long expressions of devotion.

For a variety of reasons, this exchange of words was never made a concrete love. Over and over, despite his repeated invitations, Mistral opted not to make the decisive trip from the south of Chile to Santiago to meet with Magallanes Moure, and transfigure their passion of the mind into a physical one. Perhaps she found more meaning in communication by writing than in any union of the flesh; in the letters, she also describes her ups and downs from *exaltación* (which at different moments is linked to the carnal and the spiritual) and *depresión*. In the end, she concludes, her aim is *serenidad*. Magallanes Moure, on the other hand, despite his lofty verses, was more down to earth in this respect, and one can feel his frustration at her repeated evasions of his hinting. At one point, he at last directly invites her to enjoy the straightforward pleasures of the body, but Mistral is horrified, saying she would only have him if they were surrounded by trees, in nature:

No, darling Manuel, not in a hotel. Those are sites prostituted by depraved men and easy women. I don't want to kiss you, or take you into my arms, in a place like that. I want you under the open sky, amidst trees. The fertile earth, with its special perfume that gives vigor to things, the veins, the soul, the sun, the trees, is in all ways potent and healthy, and will help your voice to awaken love in me just the way you desire it, the kind of life that today remains sleeping. Under a roof, no; in the vile atmosphere of a hotel, I wouldn't want you.

But then she goes on:

Listen: I'm lying down against a trunk. I've always liked to kiss trunks on their wounds full of pale rubber. This trunk has a *dense, black* tangle wrapped around its base, which belongs to who knows what vine. I've just kissed the trunk on its rubber-packed wound; but it's not the tree I kiss, as at other moments, it's you, my darling, you. This is your mouth. It's warm because a ray of sun has fallen onto it. This whole dead vine imitates a black beard that grazes me in a caress. Here you are, you, the one that I've kissed.

Beardly grazes notwithstanding, the relationship between these two poets went far beyond the body. Two minds found in each other a depth of thought and conversation they did not find in others around them. Even so, time took its toll. He grew frustrated by her repeated deflections and ethical qualms, which she justified as spirituality, while she came to find his way of treating her insensitive and superficial. ("Don't lie. It really isn't necessary (. . .) And don't *make me into literature*.")

The rupture came when he made his frustrations explicit and took up with another writer in Santiago, Sara Hübner, who wrote under the pseudonym Magda Sudermann. Mistral was incredibly hurt, but the two didn't entirely break contact despite this. Years later, she would recall the entire drama as an attempt to instruct Magallanes Moure toward a more spiritual way of being—at the time, however, it's certain that neither of them experienced their angst as didacticism. The nuanced letters between them are worth reading in their entirety, in the collection edited by Chile's Universidad Católica. Her romantic relationship with Doris Dana has come to light in recent decades (with the correspondence between those two recently translated into English by Velma García-Gorena) but Mistral was more complex than even that. As was Magallanes Moure. While the translation (or transmutation) of life to art is never straightforward, in this case I think the letters between the writers shed light on the stories here, in which allegiances are divided and motives are double- or triple-edged, but a sensitivity to the emotional contours of small objects or gestures can be found at even the moments of greatest disquiet.

"What is Love?", the first story, which shares a near title with the collection, is notable for its unusual setting of a printing press, where machinery clatters and a stressful deadline must be met to publish a saltpeter report ordered by the Ministry of Finance. Saltpeter is of major importance in Chile, used in a number of industrial processes, and from 1879-1884 the country went to war with Peru and Bolivia to take over their saltpeter deposits. Against this backdrop with its eye on the bottom line, Antonio falls for his colleague Paulina, portrayed as androgynous in her manner and dress, fraternizing with men and laboring alongside them; this depiction of a working woman also stands out. Here the relationship between the mechanical and the sensual is key, not just in the description of the printing press itself, but also in the way that Antonio's soul unfolds and reads the broadsheet of his emotions. Newspaper, soul, sex—the three are metaphorically bound. The motivations behind the attraction are just as mingled. It's unclear whether Antonio falls for Paulina due to her own "self" (however that might be interpreted), or due to her act of reading mystics in the tradition of Catholic literature. The two work at the same desk as copyeditors, sitting across from each other, and a constant annoyance exists between them, obvious tension. This is intensified by language, through her act of reading the assignments out loud, verses of a religious work. In her mouth the words become erotic, speaking to not just the subliminal charge of a great deal of mystic poetry, but also to how language, the gestures of the body, the words used, and the tone of voice can produce attraction. The superficial dichotomy of the printing press's hard mechanical work and the "mystery, mystery, mystery" of love holds only to a point, with the reading of literature serving as a meeting place between the two, operating its effects.

"New Year", the second story and the longest of the collection, explores deception, hope and humiliation. The borderline between one year and the next is an existential moment of change, decision, resolve, and in this case, alteration of one's understanding of an emotional situation. Magallanes Moure plays with light and shadow, with an extended use of chiaroscuro. Light transforms at the limit of shadow; one recalls his affiliation with the Los Diez group of poets and artists, as well as his training as a painter. The tale begins with Daniel leaving what is perhaps Santiago's most symbolic building, La Moneda; here is another man with a government job. "Ardent" light hits a row of closed windows, a glimpse at how desire might be blocked. But the shadowy vestibule Daniel enters suggests hopeful possibility, an opportunity for promising silence and unwitnessed contact, not threat. We mostly follow events from Daniel's free indirect perspective, which occasionally slips into omniscient commentary. ("How interested they were in keeping up appearances! As if their expectations of happiness rested on such hypocrisy.") In the actions of the various characters, the story subtly explores the threshold between deceit and truth, appearance and reality, promise and lie, adventure and boredom. Ultimately, the categories of "deception" in the outside world, and security and society at home, are destabilized, with the golden light flickering between chiaroscuro's ambiguity and absolute darkness. The last line, "a new life", remains tantalizingly enigmatic, as does Marta's refrain—"Will you always want to believe in it?"

"Summer Sun", the third story, introduces another working environment: this time, a sewing room. Magallanes Moure evokes thick heat, sun, shadow, silence. What isn't said is as important as what is, and slow gestures—the bunching of a skirt, the revelation of a leg, a yawn—take on a complicity in wordlessness. Love itself is slow here, carried out as an interminable series of social visits to a traditional middle-class Santiago home. Sewing work is done not so much to make a product—as with the newspapers—but to pass the time, and this torpor is sensual. Notably, just as in other stories, the loved woman, María, is a mother, and Samuel briefly ponders the "consequences of maternity." This brief qualm only seems to apply to her body, however, which he concludes is still as youthful as a single woman's, and there is little thought of the consequences of stealing a moment with another's wife. Once again, Magallanes Moure proposes a startling vision of love in which desire triumphs over social mores and expectations. The ending might be happy, or not; the story cuts off after the instant of achieved bliss.

"The Defense," the fourth story, takes the form of a confession—to whom, it is not quite clear. Priest? Friend? Reader? Judge? Heavenly gatekeeper? (Somewhat cryptically, the narrator says *omnia transit* is his interlocutor's motto.) The story begins with a legal defense of infidelity with a neighbor's wife, and is phrased in terms of what is "just." Innocuous speculation about a new family on the block drifts into the stirrings of a relationship. The narrator never says he's in love with the woman, but always defends himself by saying he just wanted to make her happy. Society is important here, as the narrator's wife insists to him: "Life in society is necessary. Isolation leads to illness in men like you, who work all day long. One has to go out, distract oneself, talk with people who aren't the same as those we see every day, exchange ideas . . ." But society also lays down specific regulations for friendship between a man and a woman. As in the other stories, work enters the picture—the narrator mentions "construction projects" for the Ministry of Public Works, portrayed as a relatively noble career, whereas the *nouveau riche* husband who makes his money on the stock market is made out to be devoid of spiritual substance. Again, as in previous stories, this is not love at first sight but a gradual love that builds over time, in an organic way, evoking nature. The narrator likens love to life itself, not "villainy," and questions the very terms of the prosecution keen to find him guilty. The story's fragmentary form, with its spaces, breaks, justifications and elisions, offers the perspective of the narrator alone, who is of course unreliable. (But what does it mean to be reliable?) Not only is he trying to convince the other, he is trying to convince himself. The suggestion of false consciousness, the confusion of reality and dream, and the claim of sacrifice for another's happiness confronted against the reality of mutual fulfillment, mark this story as "modern" and bring it into dialogue with literary developments in the first decades of the 20th century in Chile and beyond.

To sum up rather brutally, Magallanes Moure's stories include, in no particular order: deception, manual activities (printing, knitting, sewing, et cetera), hiddenness, theft, seductive words versus seductive physical attributes, Biblical quotes (e.g. from Solomon), artists' quotes (e.g. from Ruskin), languidness / lacklusterness / longing, wilting / weather / weariness, *qué diran* (what'll they say) and concern for others' opinions, society as stifling convention, art as salvation or the excuse to gawk at peers (e.g. at operettas), love as slow and gradual development, and contrasts between banal conversations meant to pass the time and inner monologues occasionally translated into action or literature.

"Modern". I used that word, but what does it mean? I can't say I know, but I can point to what I believe to be the most remarkable description in the book, where Magallanes Moure describes a passing tram. In the course of its movement, not only do light and shade alternate, but the fragmented stretches of conversation become the equivalent of slats of bright and dark—a verbal chiaroscuro. Daniel and Marta speak one way in the dark and another in the light when they're being spied on by her mother. Another moment of chiaroscuro: the shadows of the two move across the light-filled wall like a magic lantern, a vision of what could be. An illusion, maybe, but also a foregrounding for what could be possible, obscured in the present but perhaps one day permitted by the world that is signaled by the tram, with whatever new social innovations it brings.

The tense changes midway through the story, from the past (already over) to the infinitive (still possible). Marta suggests a complicated plan to meet at New Year's with her husband there. She'll turn around, and the two lovers will meet face to face. This dangerous ideal of a face-to-face encounter, for Magallanes Moure, suggests a true meeting with the other (just as it later will do for Emmanuel Levinas and so many thinkers). From here we cut to Daniel's family scenes with wife and children. She plays songs on the piano, a limpid and floating light valse free of dissonances. Simple and fresh Adela's soul is translated into the music

115

of Moszkowski, Grieg, Schumann. Meanwhile, Daniel enjoys the further double life and double consciousness this permits him, as he recalls lines from Flaubert, the famous ballroom scene where Emma Bovary dances with the Viscount. (Literature comes to parallel infidelity here in that both mark a betrayal of the world here and now, on behalf of a world of dream and fantasy.) The translations of Flaubert's lines, in Eleanor Marx's version, read: "They began slowly, then went more rapidly" and "On passing near the doors the bottom of Emma's dress caught against his trousers. Their legs commingled; he looked down at her; she raised her eyes to his." Interestingly, in Magallanes Moure's story, the sentence connecting these two phrases is left out: "They turned; all around them was turning—the lamps, the furniture, the wainscoting, the floor, like a disc on a pivot." But this disorientation returns later in the tale with a vengeance, as hidden cargo.

Magallanes Moure channels European sources of music and literature, but the effect is enigmatic. Although Emma dances with the elegant viscount, she does not end up with him. But who is the Madame Bovary? Is it Marta or Adela? Or does this musical evocation instead parallel Tolstoy's *Kreutzer Sonata*? (Recall

Magallanes Moure's friends and their disastrous attempt to make a Tolstoyan colony.) Once again, the subtleties of the plot are paralleled by the subtleties of the artworks and the subtleties of the emotions. An uneasy, if tender, ambiguity reigns.

※

Without presenting any utopian alternative, in these stories Magallanes Moure presents the arbitrariness of convention, and explores the phenomenology of non-heterosexual married love and its effects on the body. A sociologist might abstractly sum up his interest as the complication of transgressive love a century ago in Chile, but here the stories offer the experience itself.

The comfortable becomes strange, the light slowly dims, and the rocky path fills with unfamiliar silhouettes, outlines of trees, jags of branches . . . Magallanes Moure's stories invite the kind of speculative thinking about alternatives and mutual acceptance that the path is strange but can still be walked together that is found so often in contemporary love. More mature and less saccharine than his romantic poems, these impressionistic tales are written with a light touch but density of theme, and remain provocative. Open to interpretative ambiguity, and to many varieties of translation from their time to this one—new kinds of words, new forms of life—they offer sketches of human complexity, not answers.

—Jessica Sequeira

Further Reading

—Magallanes Moure, Manuel. *Obras completas*. Origo Ediciones, 2012.

—ed. Martínez Sanz, María Ester y Vargas Saavedra, Luis. *Manuel, en los labios por mucho tiempo. Epistolario entre Gabriela Mistral Lucila Godoy Alcayaga y Manuel Magallanes Moure*. Ediciones Universidad Católica de Chile, 2005.

—ed. Méndez, Verónica and Montero, Gonzalo. *Revista Los Diez (1916–1917)*. Editorial Cuarto Propio, 2012.

—Mistral, Gabriela. *Gabriela Mistral's Letters to Doris Dana*. University of New Mexico Press, 2018.

—Molina Núñez, Julio y Araya, Juan Agustín. *Selva lírica: estudios sobre los poetas chilenos*. Soc. Imp. y Lit. Universo, 1917.

—Prado, Pedro. *Cartas a Manuel Magallanes Moure*. Editorial Universitaria, 1986.

A PARTIAL LIST OF SNUGGLY BOOKS

MAY ARMAND BLANC *The Last Rendezvous*
G. ALBERT AURIER *Elsewhere and Other Stories*
CHARLES BARBARA *My Lunatic Asylum*
S. HENRY BERTHOUD *Misanthropic Tales*
LÉON BLOY *The Tarantulas' Parlor and Other Unkind Tales*
ÉLÉMIR BOURGES *The Twilight of the Gods*
CYRIEL BUYSSE *The Aunts*
JAMES CHAMPAGNE *Harlem Smoke*
FÉLICIEN CHAMPSAUR *The Latin Orgy*
BRENDAN CONNELL *Metrophilias*
BRENDAN CONNELL (editor)
    The Zinzolin Book of Occult Fiction
RAFAELA CONTRERAS *The Turquoise Ring and Other Stories*
DANIEL CORRICK (editor)
    Ghosts and Robbers: An Anthology of German Gothic Fiction
ADOLFO COUVE *When I Think of My Missing Head*
QUENTIN S. CRISP *Aiaigasa*
ALADY DILKE *The Outcast Spirit and Other Stories*
ÉDOUARD DUJARDIN *Hauntings*
BERIT ELLINGSEN *Now We Can See the Moon*
ERCKMANN-CHATRIAN *A Malediction*
ALPHONSE ESQUIROS *The Enchanted Castle*
ENRIQUE GÓMEZ CARRILLO *Sentimental Stories*
DELPHI FABRICE *Flowers of Ether*
DELPHI FABRICE *The Red Spider*
BENJAMIN GASTINEAU *The Reign of Satan*
EDMOND AND JULES DE GONCOURT *Manette Salomon*
REMY DE GOURMONT *From a Faraway Land*
REMY DE GOURMONT *Morose Vignettes*
GUIDO GOZZANO *Alcina and Other Stories*
GUSTAVE GUICHES *The Modesty of Sodom*
EDWARD HERON-ALLEN *The Complete Shorter Fiction*
EDWARD HERON-ALLEN *Three Ghost-Written Novels*
RHYS HUGHES *Cloud Farming in Wales*
J.-K. HUYSMANS *The Crowds of Lourdes*
J.-K. HUYSMANS *Knapsacks*
COLIN INSOLE *Valerie and Other Stories*
JUSTIN ISIS *Pleasant Tales II*

www.ingramcontent.com/pod-product-compliance
Lightning Source LLC
Chambersburg PA
CBHW050419110726
47899CB00008B/2773